The House Sitters

Written by Jill Eggleton
Illustrated by Sandra Cammell

Rigby

Bob was going away
on a vacation.
He put a poster
in the shop window.

A man came
to Bob's house.
He had a big box.
"I have come to look after
your house," he said.

"Good," said Bob.
"But what have you got
in that box?"

"Chickens," said the man.

"Chickens!" said Bob.
"I cannot have chickens
in my house."

"My chickens can't stay
in the box," said the man.
"So I can't look after
your house."
And he went away.

A woman came
to Bob's house.
She had a red truck.
"I have come to look after
your house," she said.

"Good," said Bob.
"But what have you got
in that truck?"

"Goats," said the woman.

"Goats," said Bob.
"I cannot have goats
in my house."

"My goats can't stay
in the truck," said the woman.
"So I can't look after
your house."
And she went away.

Molly called Bob
on the telephone . . .

"I can look after
your house," she said.

"Have you got chickens
or goats?" asked Bob.

"No," said Molly.
"I've got fish."

"Good," said Bob.
"The fish can stay
in their bowl.
You can look after
my house."

11

So Bob went away
and Molly came to Bob's
house in a big bus.
She had her fish in a bowl
and . . . ten kids in the bus!

And when Bob came home, he got a **big** surprise!

Posters

━━━ Guide Notes

Title: The House Sitters
Stage: Early (3) – Blue

Genre: Fiction
Approach: Guided Reading
Processes: Thinking Critically, Exploring Language, Processing Information
Written and Visual Focus: Posters
Word Count: 240

THINKING CRITICALLY
(sample questions)
- What do you think this story could be about?
- Look at pages 2 and 3. Why do you think Bob wants someone to look after his house?
- Look at pages 4 and 5. Why do you think Bob doesn't want chickens in his house?
- Look at pages 6 and 7. What could happen if Bob let goats into his house?
- Look at page 11. What do you notice about the way Bob is packing his suitcase? What sort of person do you think he is?
- Look at page 14. How do you think Bob feels? What do you think he will do?

EXPLORING LANGUAGE

Terminology
Title, cover, illustrations, author, illustrator

Vocabulary
Interest words: house sitter, bowl, poster, surprise
High-frequency words: what, so
Compound word: cannot
Positional words: in, on

Print Conventions
Capital letter for sentence beginnings and names (**B**ob, **M**olly), periods, exclamation marks, quotation marks, commas, ellipsis, question marks